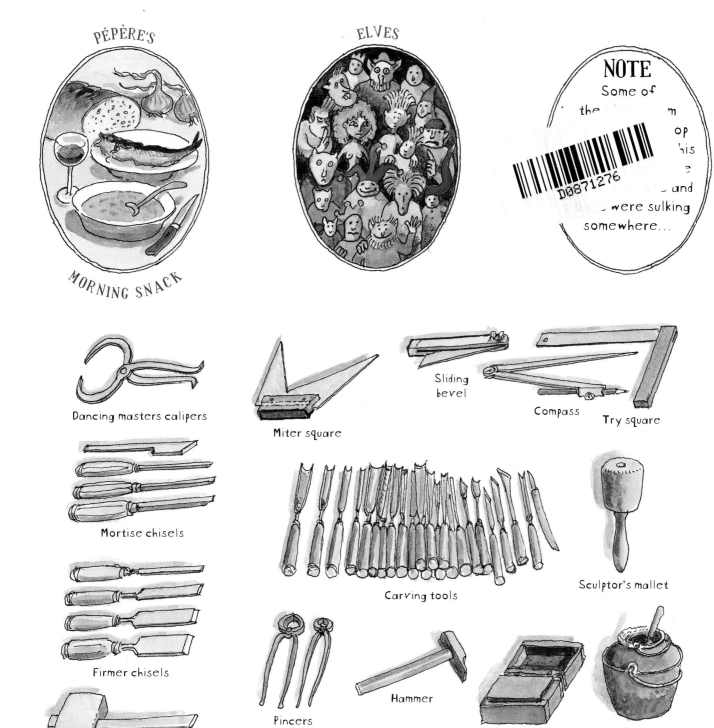

PÉPÈRE'S

MORNING SNACK

ELVES

NOTE

Some of
the   m
op
his
e
and
were sulking
somewhere...

Dancing masters calipers

Miter square

Sliding bevel

Compass

Try square

Mortise chisels

Carving tools

Sculptor's mallet

Firmer chisels

Pincers

Hammer

Sharpening stone

Glue pot

Joiner's mallet

ROBIN GROSBOIS

1894 - 1954

CHARLES GROSBOIS

1768 - ?

ABEL GROSBOIS

1770 - 1795

GRANDPA'S WORKSHOP

"DANS L'ATELIER DE PÉPÈRE"

Published by Lost Art Press LLC in 2012
26 Greenbriar Ave., Fort Mitchell, KY, 41017, USA
Web: http://lostartpress.com

Title: Grandpa's Workshop
Author: Maurice Pommier
Translator: Brian Anderson
Editors, English Edition: Christopher Schwarz and Lucy May
Editor, French Edition: Jacques van Geen
Designer: Philippe Laborde

English translation dedicated to Maia and Rachel.

First published in French by Gallimard Jeunesse in 2007 as
"DANS L'ATELIER DE PÉPÈRE."

ISBN: 978-0-9850777-2-3

First English printing.

This book was printed and bound in the United States.

GRANDPA'S WORKSHOP

Maurice Pommier

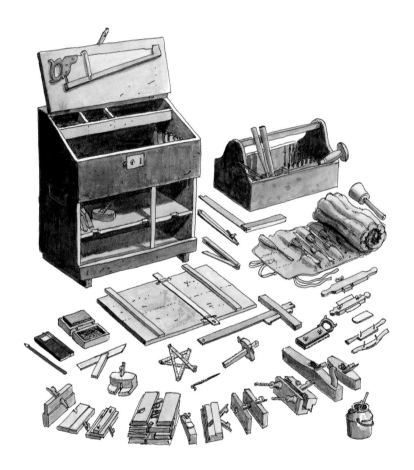

TO MY PÉPÈRE EUGÈNE, WHO I NEVER KNEW,

TO MY PÉPÈRE LÉONARD, WHO TOLD ME STORIES.

SHORT PREAMBLE

Pépère gives a jackknife to Louis. Louis uses Pépère's knife.

Louis grows. He becomes a man.

The jackknife's blade wears out, and is replaced.
Years later, it is the handle's turn to be replaced.

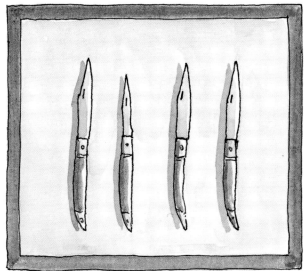 

Louis is now a grandfather. He gives Pépère's jackknife to his grandson.
Is it the same knife?

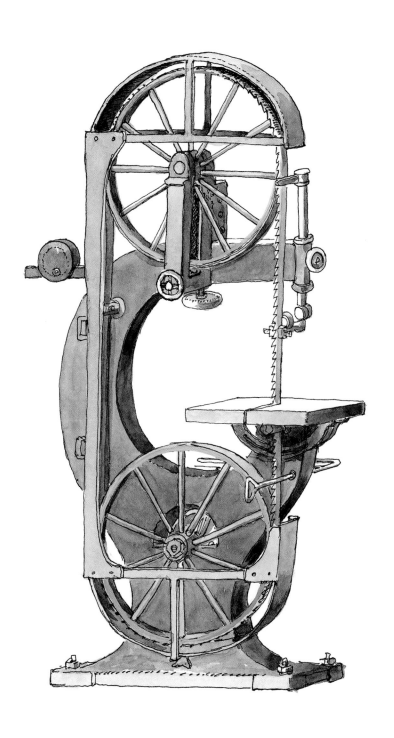

I love to go to my grandparents' house on vacation. I play in Pépère's woodshop. It is the little house at the bottom of the garden, behind the two apple trees. I go in the little door, so I can say hello to Jack-in-the-Green. He is the man with a face of leaves that Pépère carved in the door, the spirit who watches over the shop.

Pépère is a joiner. He knows how to hammer–saw–plane–rasp–sand–drill–hew–carve. He builds furniture, doors, windows and TOYS. He says his woodshop is inhabited by elves. Grandma says they are mice! Pépère loves his tools. He says they tell him many STORIES. Grandma says he is far too deaf to hear anything at all, and that he never hears when she calls him. Pépère is a joker.

I give Pépère a big hug, and then go play in the shavings until he says :
— Wow, my little rabbit, is this circus going to go on all day?
Then he asks me if I would like some nails and a hammer to play joiner or carpenter. He also gives me some scraps of wood that he pulls out of the box beside his workbench, and I build houses or boats. Sometimes I hit my fingers with the hammer... Pépère says,
— That is the skill building in you!

I ALSO WATCH him working at his bench, and he teaches me the names of the tools.

— That way, you will know when I ask you to bring me something!
He started to show me how to saw, but said that I am still a little too small.

I would really like to see the elves who live in the woodshop. I have looked long and hard, in every hidden corner, but I have never seen them.

I don't know where Pépère learned all the stories he knows.
He tells me he keeps them stored under his hat. I ask myself how they can all fit there.
He knows every step on the path the wood takes,
from the depths of the forest all the way to his workbench.
He tells me of the LOGGERS, like bearded grumpy bears, who go into the forest to cut
enormous trees. When he speaks, I hear the sound of the falling trees, the intense
crackling and crunching, and the deep silence of the forest just after. He knows the men
who skid the logs out of the forest and the teamsters who haul them to the sawmill.
He also knows a sawyer with one eye, an ear always tuned to the song of his saw...

His stories are always full of men with skilled hands who build houses, palaces, cabinets,
and even magic chests!... The stories are often full of magic : the Rabbit with the Golden
Square, the Carpenter who Cheated the Devil, an entire world of elves, mischievous or
irascible, and even terrifying basilisks, or the Vouivres, who are half woman, half snake.

THE VOUIVRE

THE RABBIT

THE CARPENTER

THE BASILISK

SVCELLVS

ESVS

Pépère loves tools. He knows how to sharpen saws, the irons of his planes, chisels and gouges. When a handle breaks, he knows how to make a new one. He knows his tools like they were members of his family.
He speaks of wonders, and can even tell you of the hammers of the Gallic gods, or the adzes used by the ancient Romans.

Pépère also loves wood. Oak, hornbeam, beech. If you walk with him in the forest, he can recognize and name all the kinds of trees. He even knows the wood when it has been cut into planks. He carries with him the scent of the woods that he works, the resin of pine, the tannin of oak — though after his snack, he smells mostly of red wine and garlic.

He wakes up early, long before even the chickens, and he doesn't have breakfast like I do, with hot chocolate, toasted bread and jam. He just gulps down a cup of coffee and goes to work. Around eight in the morning, he breaks his bread: he eats some soup, bread, smoked fish, cheese and some onion or garlic, all of it washed down with a small glass of wine. The best time to catch him to hear a good story is when he heads back to work, before he takes up his tools again.
— Pépère, tell me the story of your saw!
— Which saw, little rabbit? I have lots of them. Let's see if you know them.

I remember the lesson. There are saw blades with SMALL TEETH or BIG TEETH, and they are mounted in frames or on handles.
I told him the names of all the saws, without making a mistake :

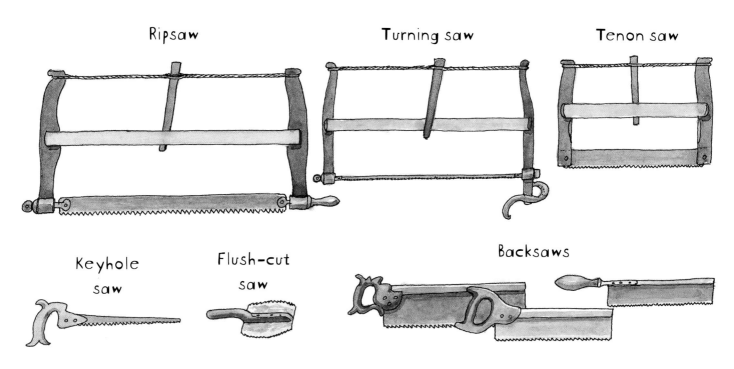

Ripsaw

Turning saw

Tenon saw

Keyhole saw

Flush-cut saw

Backsaws

And don't forget the band saw!

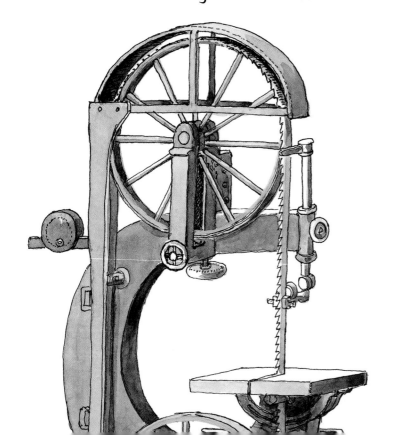

— Please tell me the story of the big English handsaw, Pépère!
— AND ZING AND ZANG, open your ears Sylvain, the saw is talking to you...

12

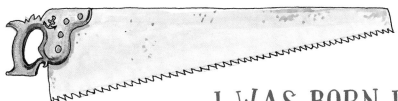

I WAS BORN IN 1820.

My first owner was an American carpenter, John Twilbil.
He bought me in the General Store of a small town, during one of his many travels.
I was made in Great Britain. And to get to the store,
I was carried by a huge ship and then some carts pulled by mules.

John Twilbil had two mules, a tool chest, a frying pan, a kettle, a big bedroll,
and a filthy character.
He wandered from worksite to worksite, and when he had earned enough money, he would
carefully put away his tools, put his mules in a livery stable, and go on a binge, spending
everything he had…

When his wallet was empty, he would get his mules and his tools, and hit the road again looking for work. He would forget his filthy character, and could work in a team, with other carpenters, to build enormous barns.

During these times, John Twilbil worked hard, he woke up and went to sleep with the chickens, he did not touch a drop of alcohol, and he ate like a giant.

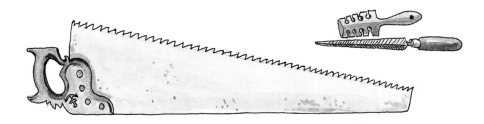

HE FILED MY TEETH VERY OFTEN, SO THAT I STAYED VERY SHARP.

He built houses, drying barns for tobacco or corn, outhouses, smokehouses, chicken coops and rabbit hutches, even sometimes fences!

MY LIFE CHANGED IN 1848.

  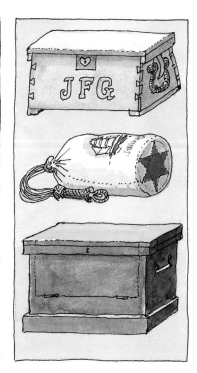

A man named James Marshal found gold in California.

GOLD !

In the blink of an eye, John Twilbil decided to sell everything he owned to go seek his fortune. I was sold to a ship's carpenter named Jean-Francois Goudron.

So I discovered the sea air, which eats any kind of steel, and the comfort of the oily cloths that my master wrapped me in to protect me.

I learned the maintenance for a ship, how to brace cargoes so that they would not shift.

Jean-François Goudron loved tattoos.
He had many on his body and on his arms.
With me, he carved a ship's anchor on my handle.
He took his time with the carving and did a good job.

He was a skillful man, and he never mistreated me.

During a stopover in Nantes, he died in his bed.

The innkeeper where he was staying
needed to pay for his funeral,
and sold all his possessions.

Clothaire Grosbois purchased me.
He was a master carpenter who traveled all over France.
Since that day, I have been passed down, father to son, and made mountains of sawdust!

— Pépère, the story of your English saw is wonderful, but did you know Clothaire Grosbois?

— Of course I knew him, I called him Pépé Clothaire. He told me the story himself!

— But how did he know that the saw belonged to an American carpenter?

— Oh, Sylvain, you know, Pépé Clothaire was a carpenter who knew his craft, one who could hear what his tools and the elves were telling him.

— BUT REALLY, PÉPÈRE, elves also live in carpenters' workshops ?...

— Of course, Pépé Clothaire himself told me of the mischievous elves who erased all his scribing lines.

— What are you talking about, "scribing lines?"

— Remember, Sylvain, when we went to his shop? Now it belongs to your Uncle Gilles. The scribing lines are what he uses to lay out and cut the wood for his trusses.

— And the elves have fun erasing them?
— The elves who lived in his workshop were musicians, yes, they were musicians and dancers. They would dance all night in the shop. But even though the elves were very light on their feet, in the morning, Pépé Clothaire could never find his lines.

Pépère picked up his tools and started working. He had finished his story.
Me, I went back to playing with the nails and scraps of wood.

I thought about the American carpenter... Did he strike gold in California?
And then I imagined all the tall ships the naval carpenter must have sailed on.

19

The darkest corner of Pépère's shop both fascinates and frightens me.
It is full of SPIDERWEBS AND DUST.
It is there that Pépère stores the tools he doesn't use anymore.

It's also the place he keeps the odds and ends of things he calls his "couldcomeinhandys."

He says it would be a terrible idea to clean the corner, because the elves would be furious.
Grandma says he should be ashamed it is such a mess,
and that he could easily clean up that shambles. Pépère just chuckles.

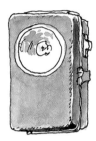

Today, I came earlier than usual.
I brought a flashlight to look through the jumble of things in the corner while
Pépère had gone to break his bread.
I discovered a big blue chest. When Pépère came back into the shop,
I tugged on his sleeve and asked him what it was.

– It's Pépé Clothaire's tool chest, he said,
tapping his finger on the chest.

– TOOL CHEST ?!?

– Pépé Clothaire's chest was handed down from his grandfather,
and certainly from the grandfather of his grandfather!

Pépère wrinkles his nose a bit, and he tugs on his mustache.

– Wow! It must be incredibly old!
Open it! Show me what is inside!

Pépère goes to the key board on the wall and picks up a little key among the many hanging
on nails there, and he makes a little space around the chest. He turns on the light and with
a broom sweeps the dust off the top of the chest. The key goes CRIC-CRAC in the lock.

When he opens the chest, Pépère's eyes shine.
He shows me the underside of the top where the big English saw had been stored. Then
he pulls out the tools and arranges them on the floor of the shop, and he teaches me the
names of them all :

21

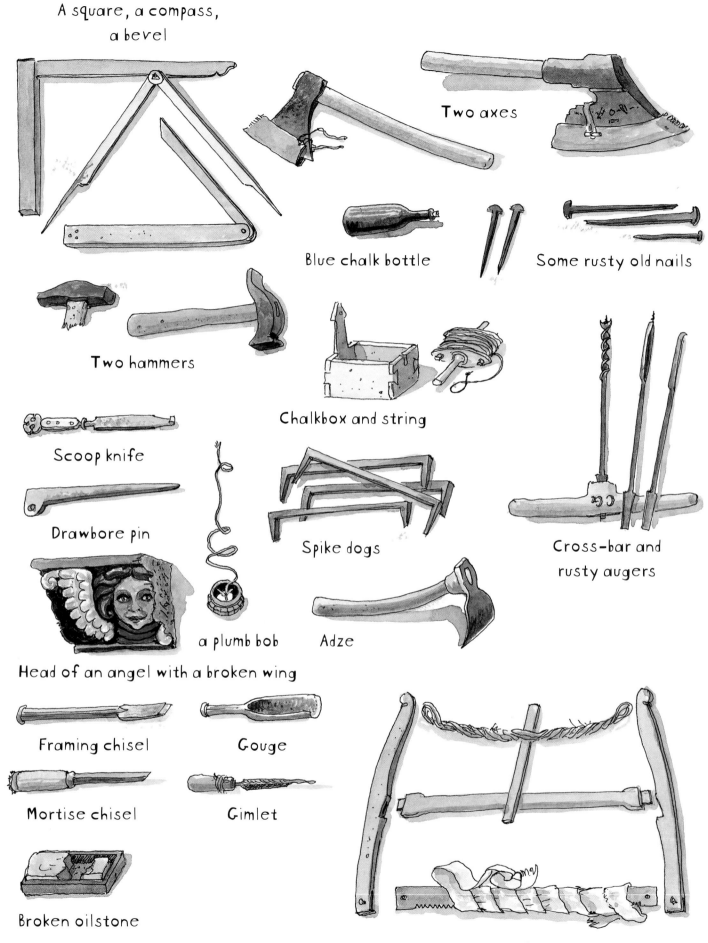

A square, a compass,
a bevel

Two axes

Blue chalk bottle

Some rusty old nails

Two hammers

Chalkbox and string

Cross-bar and
rusty augers

Scoop knife

Drawbore pin

Spike dogs

a plumb bob

Adze

Head of an angel with a broken wing

Framing chisel

Gouge

Mortise chisel

Gimlet

Broken oilstone

Dismantled frame saw

22

— Wow, Pépère, they are a little rusty...
— Yes, and they are covered with dust that tickles your nose. You see, here are almost all of your Pépé Clothaire's tools, all that he needed to build the roof structures of churches, of castles, and of houses. But there is one missing... Wait a second, I think that it is over here, it was too long to fit in the chest.

He wipes his nose and rummages around in a corner of the woodshop.
He returns, peeling oily rags off a long, strange tool.

— It is the BESAIGUË of Pépé Clothaire, Pépère tells me before I can ask him what it is. The ends of the tool are protected by leather sheaths. He takes them off to show me :

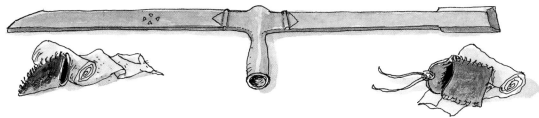

— On one end you have a big chisel, like a slick, and on the other a mortise chisel. To cut a mortise, the carpenter would drill a series of holes into a beam, and then use the besaigue to finish the square hole in the wood. He also used it to shape the pegs used to pin the joints, and when he wanted to show off, he would even use it to sharpen his pencil!

Pépère shows me how he can use the besaigue to shape a peg from a scrap of oak.
— Pépère, who did the besaigue belong to, before Pépé Clothaire?
Pépère's face falls a little, and he says that he will tell me about it later. Because he needs to put the tools away, because he has some work to do, and he isn't going to do it alone. I help him put Clothaire's tools back in the chest. Pépère takes the angel's head and looks at it, frowning, and stuffs it down deep into the chest.

That night, I had a nightmare. I was being chased by geese, and I had nothing to defend myself except Pépé Clothaire's broad axe. I kept trying to take the leather sheath off the head, but I couldn't untie the laces. A sorceress on a goat galloped after me and cried out a magic spell to try to help me.

The geese had almost caught me. I was exhausted, breathless, and couldn't run any more... I woke up after I fell out of my bed.

In the morning, in Pépère's woodshop, I didn't want to play.
I just sat on my little bench.

I asked myself why Pépère had such bright eyes yesterday when he opened the chest.

— So, little rabbit, you don't want to build something?
You look a little out of sorts!

He picked me up
and sat me on his workbench. He said :
— SSKRIC and SSKRAC !
Open your ears, Sylvain, and
listen to the story of the besaigue!

L ong ago, dwarves lived in the Black Forest. Salomon the carpenter would go there to look for trees to build houses. He was very careful not to step on the little people of the forest, and when he happened to run across one, he made sure he did not catch their eye. He was also careful not to mislay his tools or his knife, because the dwarves were always looking for metal. They were extraordinary blacksmiths and always needed metal. They forged swords for many renowned knights. Anybody who forgot an axe or a saw in the Black Forest had no chance of finding it again.

D uring every Festival of Light, Salomon would take sweets and cakes into the forest and leave them for the little people at the foot of a giant oak tree, because everybody knew that the dwarves adored honey and pastries. They also loved gold, silver, and gems. They loved the pretty colors of these metals, and the shimmer of light in the crystals left them hypnotized with pleasure. They had these treasures in every one of their underground houses, and they also hid them in abandoned burrows.

OF course, these hidden treasures excited the greed of many who lived around the forest. But the dwarves cast terrible spells on those who tried to steal from them and made them disappear forever.

Dragomir the dragon heard of the dwarves' treasures and decided to steal them. He went to the Black Forest and started to rend and tear the earth with his powerful claws, pulling trees out by their roots

and tossing aside boulders. The dwarves saved themselves by going down deep into the heart of the earth. Their spells were useless against this invader who threatened their lives and destroyed their homes. Yet for all his fury and roaring, Dragomir found nothing! But nobody could enter the forest. Salomon the carpenter could not work. One fine morning he got angry and decided to confront the monster. "I am not going to let some scaly overgrown chicken ruin my life!" He grabbed his axe, his mortise chisel, and his framer's chisel, and he went to tell the dragon what he thought of the situation.

— I WOULD BE HAPPY

if you would go breathe somewhere else! Salomon cried at the dragon. Dragomir stopped ripping up the earth to see who dared speak to him. Furious, he rushed with a roar at Salomon, who dodged away and gave him a mighty blow with the axe.

The fight was terrible. With every assault, the dragon swiped the small man with its paws. Salomon slashed back with his axe. The dragon's claws ripped up Salomon's clothes and drew blood. The forest floor was covered with blood and scales that glinted in the light! Suddenly, Dragomir, with a swipe of his mighty paw, jerked the axe from Salomon and jammed the carpenter against a tree. The dragon growled: I am going to smash you, little worm. Your death will be slow, because you have angered me and wounded me!

Terrified and choking on the dragon's stinking, sulfurous breath, he managed to twist himself around and draw the chisels he had tucked into his belt. Salomon the carpenter drove the chisels into the little piggy eyes of the dragon.

The earth shook, and then a deep silence fell
in the Black Forest. Dragomir was dead.
The dwarves came out of their hiding places
and hailed the dragon slayer.
The king of the dwarves offered him gold,
but Salomon didn't want it. He told the king:
— You, the king of the grand forge,
make me instead a great tool!
The king took the chisels out of the eyes
of the dragon and took them down to his forge.

Three days later, a parade of dwarves came
to give the besaigue to the carpenter.
They were singing:

"Glory to Salomon, the great carpenter!
Let us celebrate the dragon slayer!
Here is the besaigue, that the king forged
It cuts, it pares, the carpenter's sword!"

The besaigue passed down from hand to hand through the centuries. Jacques Brise-Copeau had the strange idea to add a handle to the tool.

His descendant Jean Coupe-Fil gave it to Jérome Fait-Quartier. In fact it spent most of its time in the hands of Jérome's youngest son, who became a fine artisan. His father preferred to make sure that his wine skin made it safely to work every day!

After many, many years of work, and being sharpened often, the besaigue was worn out. It was Jean Machefer, the toolmaker, who rebuilt it for Pépè Clothaire.

He made a new chisel and a new mortise chisel, and then forge-welded them to the old tool's shaft. The sparks flew and the anvil rang, singing the old song, "It cuts, it pares, the carpenter's sword!"

— Pépère, you are a joiner, but you also know the stories of the carpenter's tools?

— Lots of joiners are also carpenters. The main difference is simply the size of the pieces of wood that they use! And you know, in our family, we all work wood.

— For how long?

Pépère tugged a bit on his mustache :

— Could well be since Noah, the patriarch, built his Ark, he said laughing. Rabbit, it is high time that I tell you about our ancestors.

All of them had shavings or sawdust on their clothes. You will see, growing up, you will feel their presence inside you. Cabinetmakers, joiners, carpenters, wagon wrights, loggers, clog makers, coopers, all worked wood.

All of these good men, and the women who shared their lives, we carry them inside us. Your mother, her brother Gaspard, you and me, we form one of the branches of this GRAND TREE.

— But, tell me, Pépère, my mother, did she really have two brothers? There is Uncle Gaspard, the cabinetmaker, but the other?

Pépère did not respond.

The next morning, I wasn't late getting out to see Pépère. I was happy because I was going for a ride in Leon's LITTLE TRUCK.
Pépère had finished a cupboard and was going to deliver it to his client.

As I arrived, Leon and Pépère were loading the finished piece and the small tool chest into the truck.
— Little rabbit, let's hit the road!

I was sandwiched between Pépère and Leon. The motor of the little truck made so much noise that I almost needed to shout.
— Tell me, Pépère, how long can a tool live?
— Some of them can get to be very old! The toolmakers and blacksmiths know how to replace worn metal parts with new ones, and woodworkers know how to make handles and frames and plane stocks. Then, hop! The tool is ready for another life.
It used to be that the tools were handed down from grandfather to grandson or from uncle to nephew. You could also get a gift of one or a few tools from somebody, from your family or a close friend. These gifts formed the beginning of your tool kit, and when you could afford it, you would buy others.

When I was young, I went to a hardware store to buy blades and irons.
I was the one who made the handles for the chisels and gouges,
the frames for saws, and the stocks for planes.
Some of my tools are not in their first lives. In my small chest, beside the cupboard we
are going to deliver, there is a BRACE AND BITS that are very old...
But first, tell me, what do we do with it?
— It's to drill holes, Pépère! With the right bit, of course, and without forgetting to clamp a
piece of wood behind the hole so that it doesn't break out at the back of the board!
— Bravo, rabbit! I bought another brace, a modern one with a ratchet, but somehow I have
always preferred the old one!
— Come on, Pépère, tell me how it came to live in your tool chest.
— OK, whet your ears :

— CREAK, CREAK, I am the brace in Pépère's tool chest,
and I am going to tell you where I came from.

I arrived in Robin Grosbois's shop to replace a very old brace, the one that lives now in the 'couldcomeinhandy' tools in the dark corner of the shop. It was so worn that it was almost unusable!

Robin was young, and he bought me with a bunch of other tools from the widow of a joiner who made everything that the people in his tiny village needed, from the cradle to the coffin. I wasn't in great shape when Robin acquired me.

My grip was worn out, and my poor head was riddled with worm holes.

R obin was kind of disorganized, his shop was always a mess, he spent a lot of time looking for things. But he was a fine joiner and his order book was always full.

One day, he read the army mobilization list on the wall of city hall. The last night before he went to the war, he carefully put away his tools, and swept out his woodshop.

The next morning, he went off to fight in World War I.
Everybody said the war would not last long.

But, in fact, it was the start of four long years of bloody misery and death.

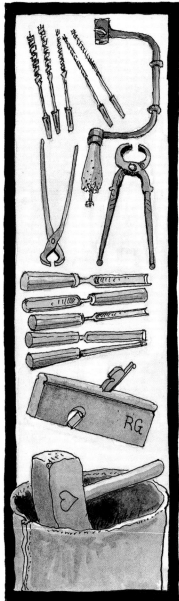

R obin escaped death and came home, but he left his hands and the right side of his face between two trenches, somewhere in the east of France.

He returned one time to his woodshop. He stayed several hours there, beside his workbench. This must have been the moment that he decided he refused to see his tools rusting and covered with dust.

He asked his daughter and his wife to pack his tools into different parcels to give away to people he liked.

I found myself in a sack with my bits, some pincers, chisels, a rabbet plane, and a mallet.

We went to the youngest of his relatives.

<big>T</big>hat was how I found
myself in Pépère's tool chest.
I was in bad shape. Most others would have tossed me in the trash or sold me for scrap...

He visited a chairmaker, working in the forest among a grove of beech trees, who
turned a new head and handle on his spring pole lathe. Pépère stripped the rust off me and
sharpened my bits, and I started on a new life with his other tools!

– WHAT A STORY !

said Leon, but we had arrived.
The couple was waiting for us.

The CUPBOARD was moved
into its place.
The clients admired Pépère's work.
They were happy to have such a
beautiful piece of furniture.

The woman said :
— The cupboard must really want
to live with us now, and she smiled.
Pépère too.

Everybody was sitting around the
table. The adults drank a glass of
rosé wine while eating crackers,
and I drank a glass of grenadine.

They gave the money to Pépère.
— Mr. Grosbois, you are an artist,
the man told him while shaking
his hand.
— No, simply a good artisan,
Pépère responded.

In the cab of the little truck, I asked :
— What happened with Robin, afterwards?
— He received a pension as a wounded veteran.
He suffered greatly from his wounds,
and he could not stand to stay in one place.

The floor of his house seemed to burn his feet.
He used to go on long walks with his wife...

They walked miles and miles and miles, those two!

Pépère is amazing. He notices immediately when there is something bothering me.
— Tell me Sylvain, why is your face so troubled this morning?
— Last night, in my sleep, the WOODSHOP ELVES came to tell me a story. It's horrible, and I can't get it out of my head. They made me promise not to tell anybody, and said if I did they would turn me into wood.

Yes, yes, they would turn me into a piece of wood...

— Oh, oh, I am going to have to have a few words with them. If they are going to threaten my grandson, they are going to find out how angry I can get!

40

So Pépère told me to go see Grandma, so that she could give me a piece of CHOCOLATE while he got things sorted out with the elves.

When I came back munching on the chocolate, Pépère told me he had laid down the law :
— I told them they were going to have to find somewhere else to live if they didn't stop threatening you. It's done. You don't have to worry, tell me what they said.
— You're sure?
— Absolutely, completely sure.
— It was terrible. They told me the story of the broken hammer
in Pépé Clothaire's tool chest.
— Ah, ha! So for once you are going to tell me a story.
— No, Pépère, I'm afraid, it is Abel's hammer, you see.
— Come on, get on with it. Say the MAGIC WORDS !
— PIM-PAM ! Your ears are mine, Pépère!

— I AM ABEL GROSBOIS' HAMMER...

41

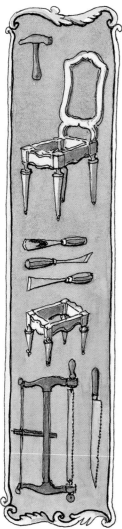

Abel Grosbois was a chairmaker
and worked with his brother Charles.
They made armchairs, stools,
couches, and chairs.

Their workshop was famous.
The wealthiest people in the kingdom
ordered furniture from them,
and noble posteriors
rested in their chairs.

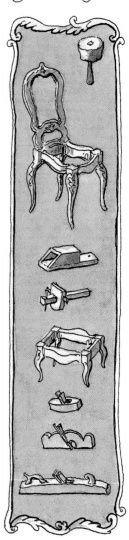

At that time, my steel was shiny,
and my handle was polished.

After Abel had finished his day,
he would put me away with his other tools
in the case under his workbench.
Charles and Abel
did not get along at all,
and they were constantly arguing.

Oddly, their work didn't suffer because of this. Wood scraps flew across the shop all the time, but for some reason, although they were extremely talented chairmakers, they couldn't throw very straight!

One afternoon, Charles came back to work stumbling. At lunch he had drunk too much.

Charles wanted to use his hammer, but couldn't put his hand on it.
He walked over to Abel's bench to borrow his brother's hammer.
Abel shoved him away and sent the tool tumbling to the floor :
— You'll just have to use your own! I will not have you putting your dirty paws on my tools!

The daily argument took a new turn.

They started to hit each other and went rolling on the floor fighting.
Abel was stronger than Charles, and that day really wanted to strangle his brother.
Charles Grosbois managed to break free and grabbed me, me, the poor hammer, where I had
lain in the shavings and sawdust on the floor. In his rage, he hit Abel many times.

His brother stopped moving, but Charles kept hitting him. My handle broke. Suddenly sober, Charles stopped and looked at his brother's body. He took Abel into his arms and shook him as if he could squeeze life back into the body! What had he done? He fled the shop, chased by his shame, anguish, and fear.

NO ONE EVER SAW HIM AGAIN.
Some people said that he took passage on a ship for Louisiana or Brazil.

It was one of Abel's sons who took over the business, and then one of his nephews...

Everybody knew my history, and nobody was proud of it, but somehow nobody ever wanted to toss me in the trash. And I, the hammer with a broken handle, moved from chest to chest down the generations, and now I live in Pépé Clothaire's tool chest...

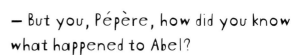

Pépère watched me with a strange expression. He ran his fingers through my hair, and he said, in the softest voice :

— That's the story...
— But I woke up just afterward! Tell me, nobody ever tried to make a new handle for the hammer?
— Ah, you know little rabbit, I don't think so. That DAMMED HAMMER has always skulked around in the tool chest of some member of our family. But understand, really, that it is the men who decide how tools are to be used.
And always remember, that drunkenness and anger never give birth to good things.

— But you, Pépère, how did you know what happened to Abel?
— When I was a little boy, I asked Pépé Clothaire why this hammer's handle had never been replaced.
— And you, did you also ask Pépé Clothaire how he knew the story?
— Pépé Clothaire told me that the elves in his shop taught him the story.

So the hammer stayed in Pépé Clothaire's tool chest, and after he died, nobody used his tools, except for the American carpenter's big saw. It was your mother's brother who used these tools.

— It wasn't Uncle Gaspard, he has all modern tools in his joinery shop. What was his name, my uncle you never want to talk about?

— Étienne... He was our first boy. We had three children, Gaspard and your mother were his brother and sister. He had a tragic accident.

HE was a carpenter and fell from the top of a church while rebuilding the roof beams. He braced his foot on the ANGEL'S HEAD in the chest. The piece broke out from under him, an angel that didn't do his job.

Since the accident, his chest has never been opened. Tools sleep and die if nobody uses them. You have woken them up a little.

Pépère told me that story quickly, without looking at me.

47

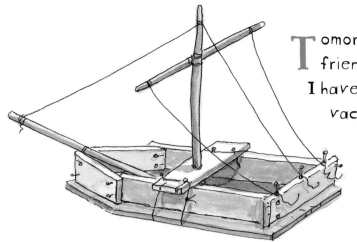

Tomorrow it is back to school. I am going to see my friends again, but I will not see Pépère as much. I have to hurry. I need to finish my BOAT before vacation ends.

    — You are well on the way to becoming a boatbuilder!

    — No, Pépère, later, I want to be a joiner, like you, and I will work with your tools!

    — Rabbit, I am really happy to hear you tell me that. If you want to become a joiner, I will show you how to use the tools little by little. But you also have to learn to work with the MACHINES like those in your Uncle Gaspard's shop. You will not work alone, like us, and not in the same way.

In the meantime, tomorrow, there is school, and that is also very important to become a good woodworker.

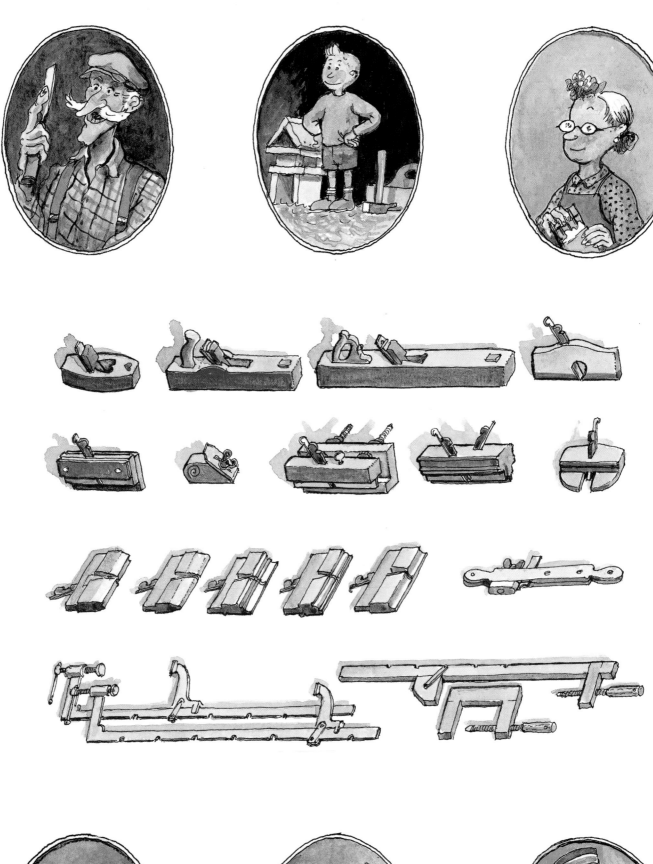